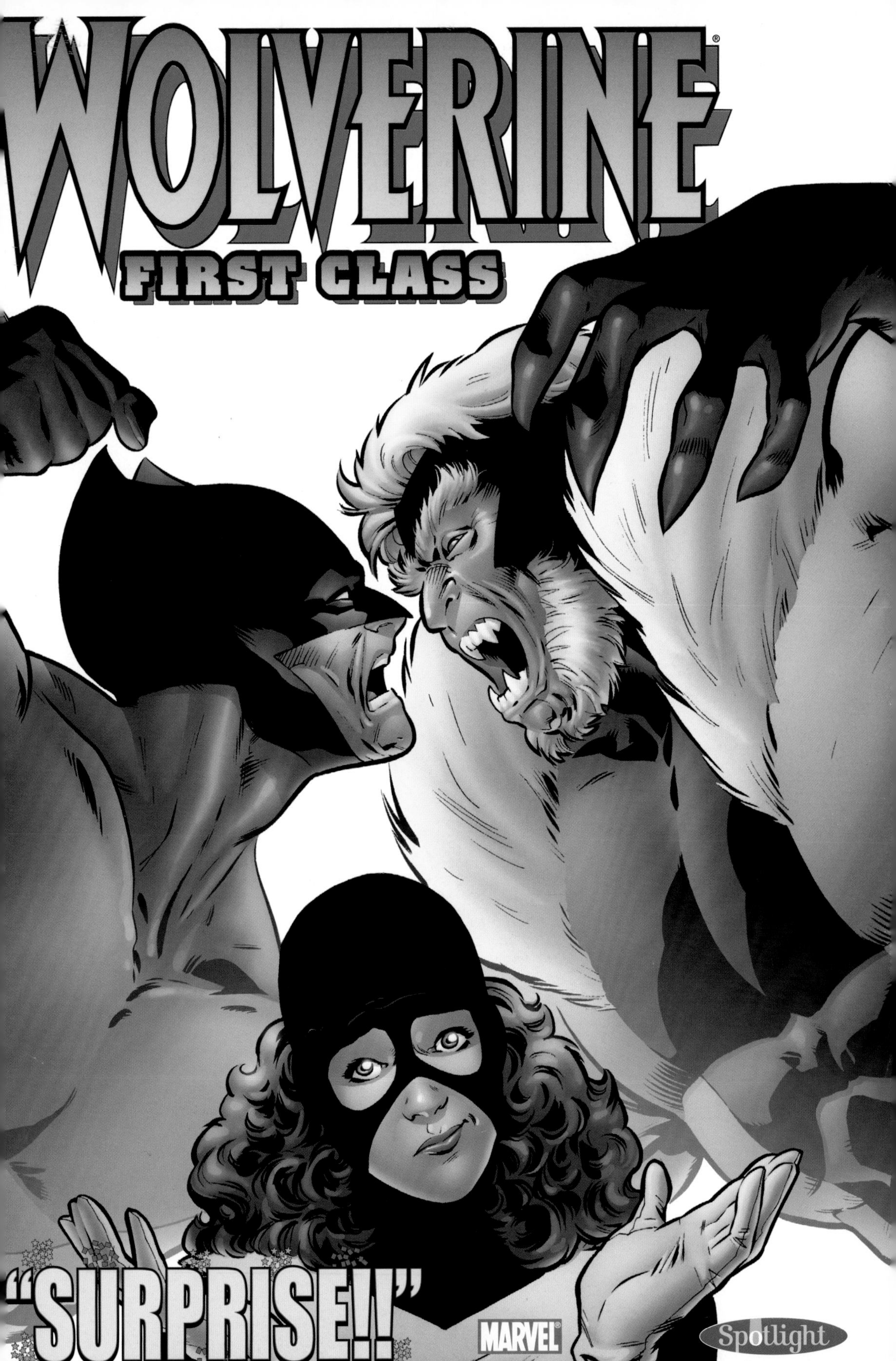
WOLVERINE
FIRST CLASS
"SURPRISE!!"
MARVEL
Spotlight
was brought to you by...

FRED VAN LENTE - WRITER
ANDREA DI VITO - ARTIST

LAURA VILLARI - COLORIST
SIMON BOWLAND - LETTERER
KIRK & BAUMANN - COVER
ANTHONY DIAL - PRODUCTION

NATHAN COSBY - ASSISTANT EDITOR
MARK PANICCIA - EDITOR
JOE QUESADA - EDITOR IN CHIEF
DAN BUCKLEY - PUBLISHER

VISIT US AT
www.abdopublishing.com

Reinforced library bound edition published in 2010 by Spotlight, a division of the ABDO Group, 8000 West 78th Street, Edina, Minnesota 55439. Spotlight produces high-quality reinforced library bound editions for schools and libraries. Published by agreement with Marvel Characters, Inc.

Library of Congress Cataloging-in-Publication Data

Van Lente, Fred.
  Surprise!! / Fred Van Lente, writer ; Andrea Di Vito, artist ; Laura Villari, colorist ; Simon Bowland, letterer.
      p. cm. -- (Wolverine, first class)
  "Marvel."
  ISBN 978-1-59961-674-2
  1. Graphic novels. 2. Graphic novels. [1. Graphic novels. 2. Superheroes--Fiction.] I. Di Vito, Andrea, ill. II. Villari, Laura. III. Bowland, Simon. IV. Title.
  PZ7.7.V26Su 2009
  741.5'973--dc22

                                    2009010139

All Spotlight books have reinforced library bindings and are manufactured in the United States of America.

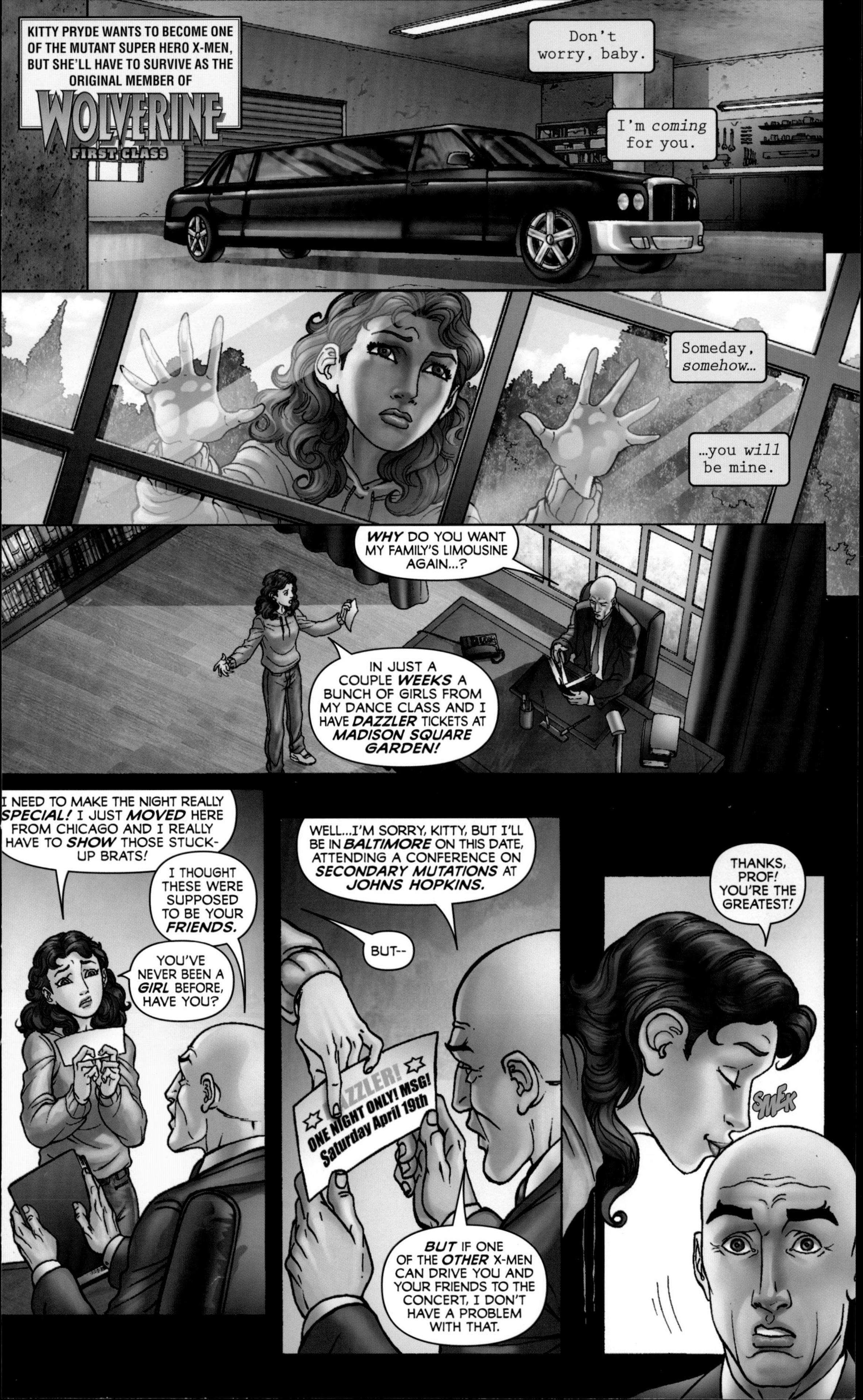
KITTY PRYDE WANTS TO BECOME ONE OF THE MUTANT SUPER HERO X-MEN, BUT SHE'LL HAVE TO SURVIVE AS THE ORIGINAL MEMBER OF
WOLVERINE FIRST CLASS
Don't worry, baby.
I'm *coming* for you.
Someday, *somehow*...
...you *will* be mine.
WHY DO YOU WANT MY FAMILY'S LIMOUSINE AGAIN...?
IN JUST A COUPLE ***WEEKS*** A BUNCH OF GIRLS FROM MY DANCE CLASS AND I HAVE ***DAZZLER*** TICKETS AT ***MADISON SQUARE GARDEN!***
I NEED TO MAKE THE NIGHT REALLY ***SPECIAL!*** I JUST ***MOVED*** HERE FROM CHICAGO AND I REALLY HAVE TO ***SHOW*** THOSE STUCK-UP BRATS!
I THOUGHT THESE WERE SUPPOSED TO BE YOUR ***FRIENDS.***
YOU'VE NEVER BEEN A ***GIRL*** BEFORE, HAVE YOU?
WELL...I'M SORRY, KITTY, BUT I'LL BE IN ***BALTIMORE*** ON THIS DATE, ATTENDING A CONFERENCE ON ***SECONDARY MUTATIONS*** AT ***JOHNS HOPKINS.***
BUT--
DAZZLER! ONE NIGHT ONLY! MSG! Saturday April 19th
BUT IF ONE OF THE ***OTHER*** X-MEN CAN DRIVE YOU AND YOUR FRIENDS TO THE CONCERT, I DON'T HAVE A PROBLEM WITH THAT.
THANKS, PROF! YOU'RE THE GREATEST!
SMEK

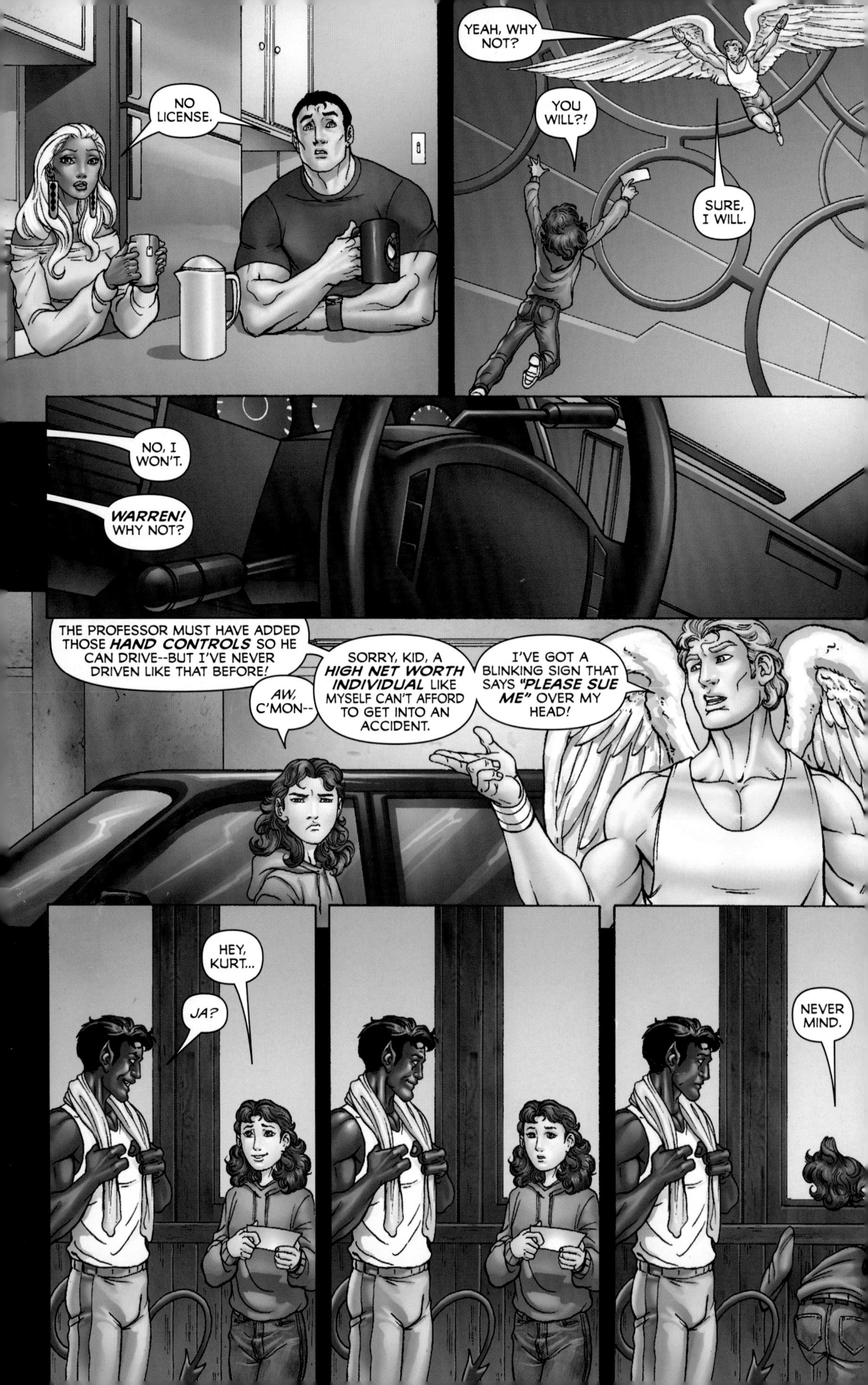
NO LICENSE.
YEAH, WHY NOT?
YOU WILL?!
SURE, I WILL.
NO, I WON'T.
WARREN! WHY NOT?
THE PROFESSOR MUST HAVE ADDED THOSE HAND CONTROLS SO HE CAN DRIVE--BUT I'VE NEVER DRIVEN LIKE THAT BEFORE!
AW, C'MON--
SORRY, KID, A HIGH NET WORTH INDIVIDUAL LIKE MYSELF CAN'T AFFORD TO GET INTO AN ACCIDENT.
I'VE GOT A BLINKING SIGN THAT SAYS "PLEASE SUE ME" OVER MY HEAD!
HEY, KURT...
JA?
NEVER MIND.

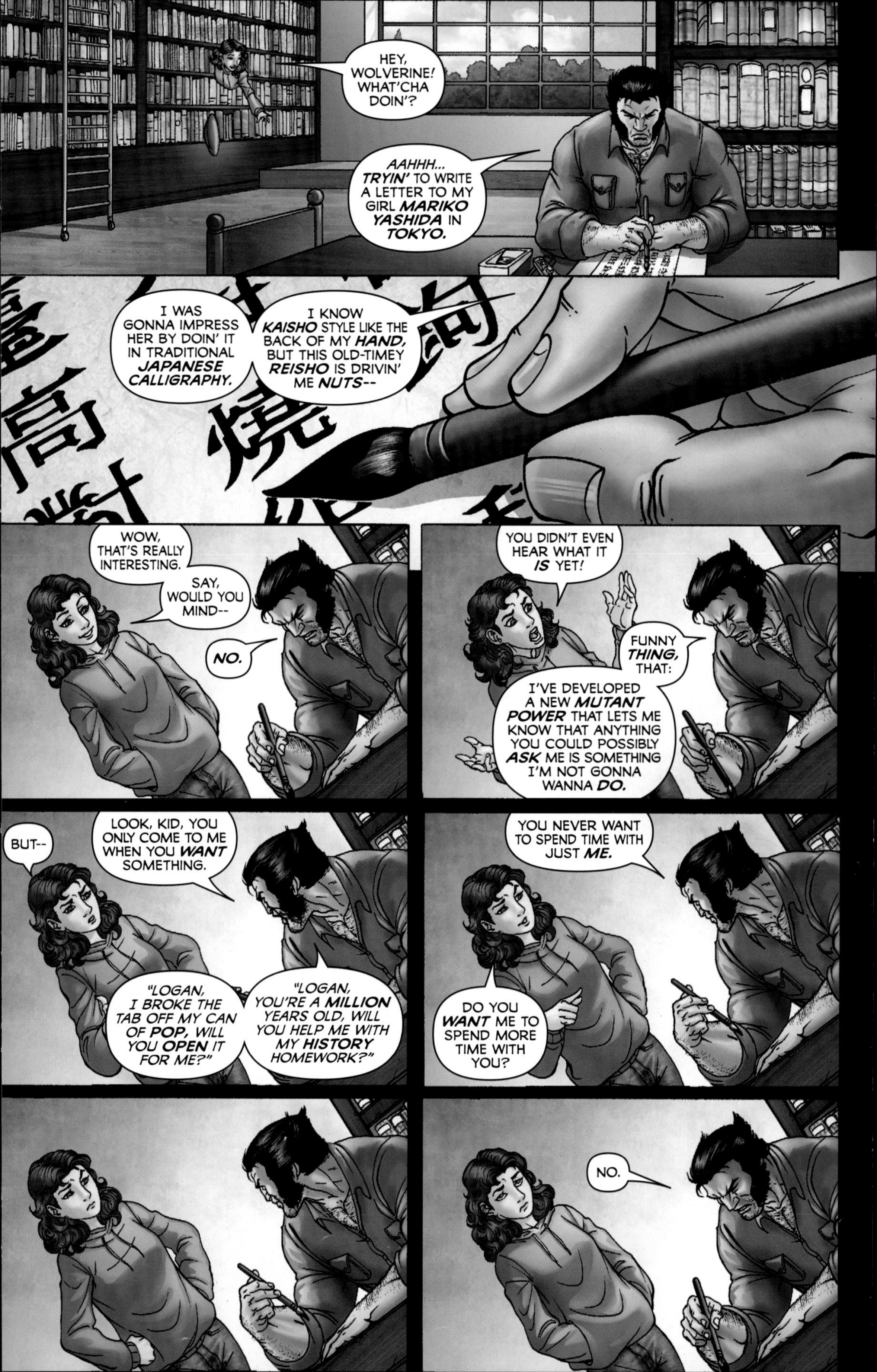
HEY, WOLVERINE! WHAT'CHA DOIN'?
AAHHH... TRYIN' TO WRITE A LETTER TO MY GIRL MARIKO YASHIDA IN TOKYO.
I WAS GONNA IMPRESS HER BY DOIN' IT IN TRADITIONAL JAPANESE CALLIGRAPHY.
I KNOW KAISHO STYLE LIKE THE BACK OF MY HAND, BUT THIS OLD-TIMEY REISHO IS DRIVIN' ME NUTS--
WOW, THAT'S REALLY INTERESTING.
SAY, WOULD YOU MIND--
NO.
YOU DIDN'T EVEN HEAR WHAT IT IS YET!
FUNNY THING, THAT:
I'VE DEVELOPED A NEW MUTANT POWER THAT LETS ME KNOW THAT ANYTHING YOU COULD POSSIBLY ASK ME IS SOMETHING I'M NOT GONNA WANNA DO.
BUT--
LOOK, KID, YOU ONLY COME TO ME WHEN YOU WANT SOMETHING.
"LOGAN, I BROKE THE TAB OFF MY CAN OF POP, WILL YOU OPEN IT FOR ME?"
"LOGAN, YOU'RE A MILLION YEARS OLD, WILL YOU HELP ME WITH MY HISTORY HOMEWORK?"
YOU NEVER WANT TO SPEND TIME WITH JUST ME.
DO YOU WANT ME TO SPEND MORE TIME WITH YOU?
NO.

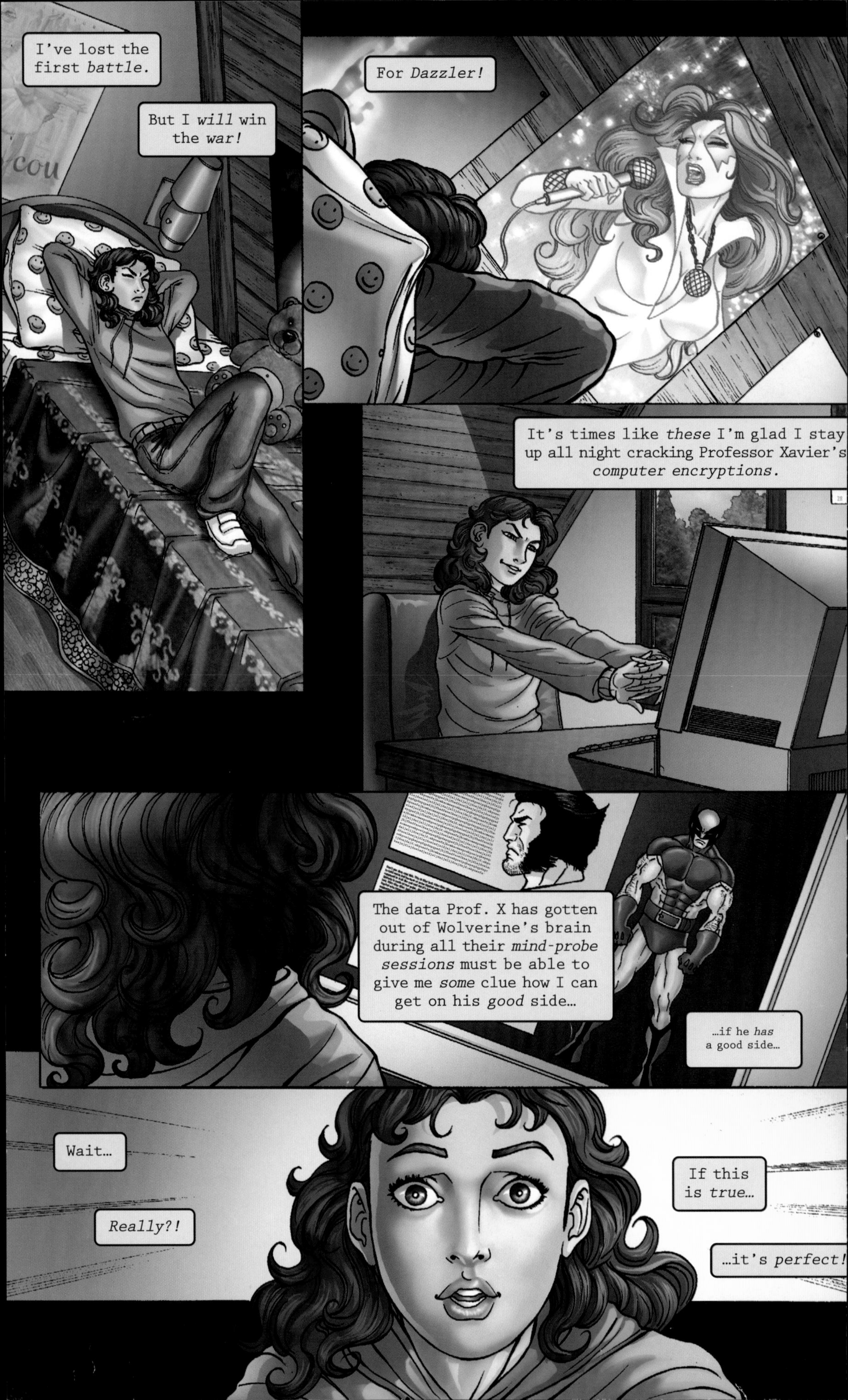
I've lost the first *battle.*
But I *will* win the *war!*
For *Dazzler!*
It's times like *these* I'm glad I stay up all night cracking Professor Xavier's *computer encryptions.*
The data Prof. X has gotten out of Wolverine's brain during all their *mind-probe sessions* must be able to give me *some* clue how I can get on his *good* side...
...if he *has* a good side...
Wait...
Really?!
If this is *true...*
...it's *perfect!*

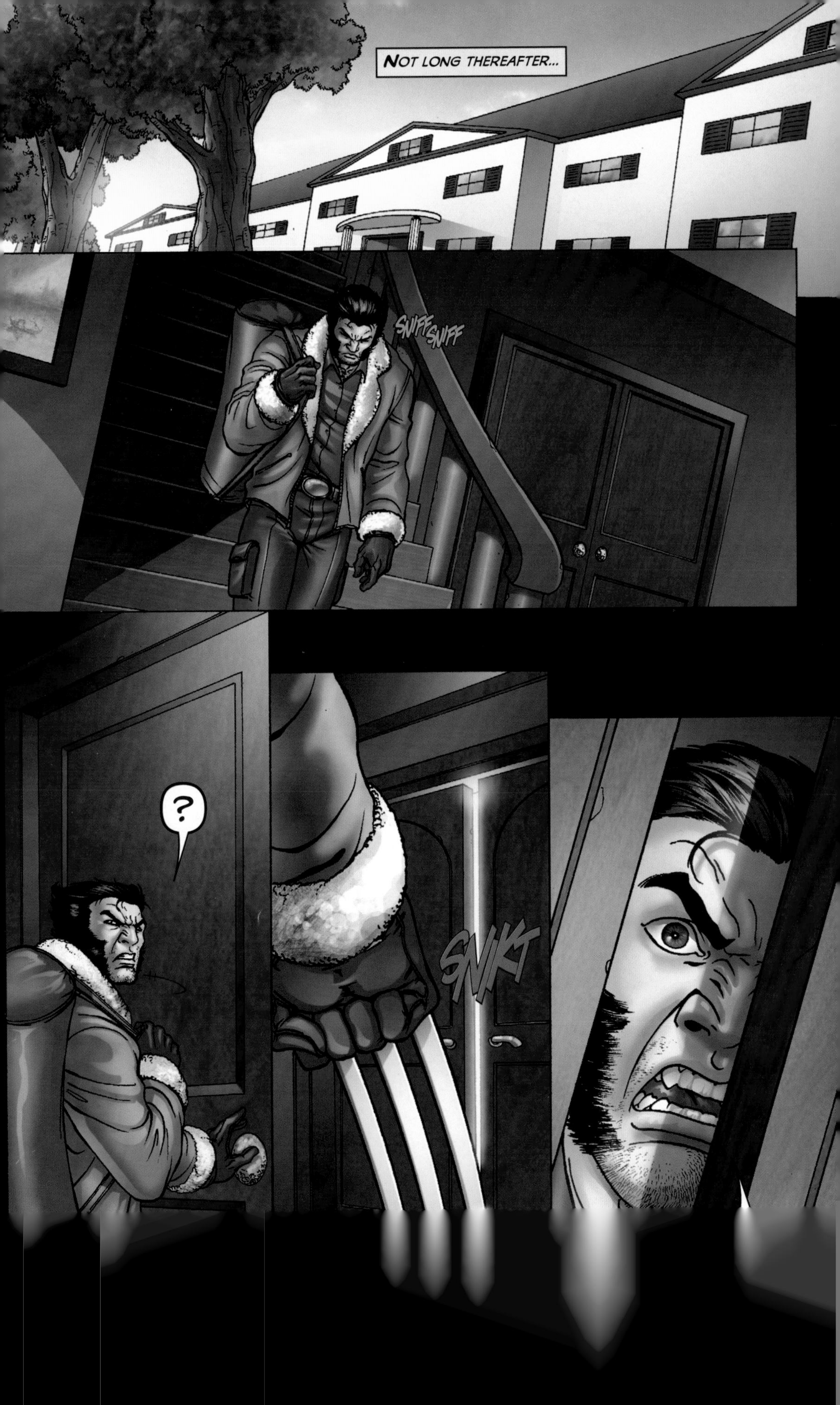

NOT LONG THEREAFTER...
SNIFF SNIFF
?
SNIKT

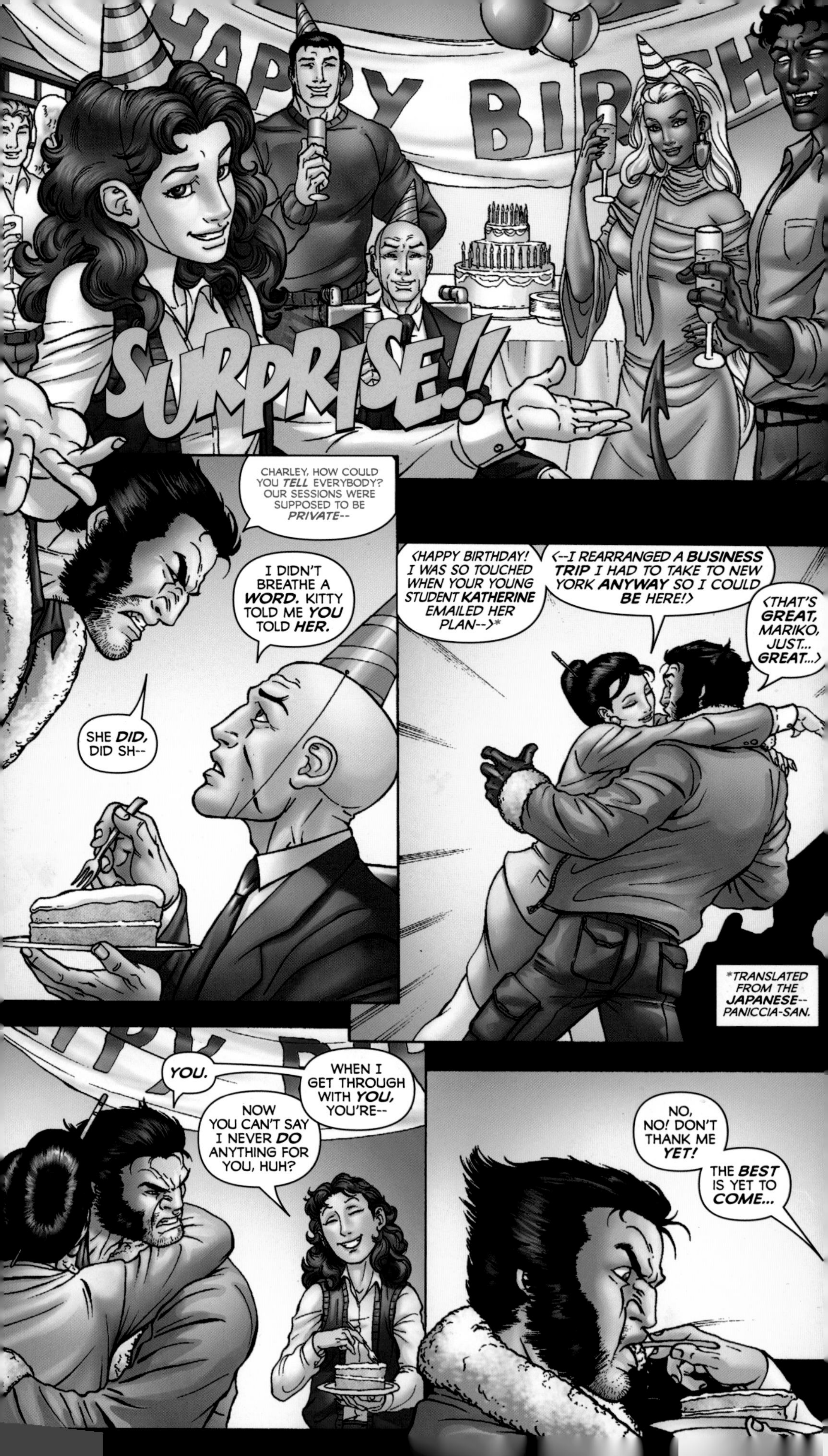
SURPRISE!!
CHARLEY, HOW COULD YOU TELL EVERYBODY? OUR SESSIONS WERE SUPPOSED TO BE PRIVATE--
I DIDN'T BREATHE A WORD. KITTY TOLD ME YOU TOLD HER.
SHE DID, DID SH--
<HAPPY BIRTHDAY! I WAS SO TOUCHED WHEN YOUR YOUNG STUDENT KATHERINE EMAILED HER PLAN-->*
<--I REARRANGED A BUSINESS TRIP I HAD TO TAKE TO NEW YORK ANYWAY SO I COULD BE HERE!>
<THAT'S GREAT, MARIKO, JUST... GREAT...>
*TRANSLATED FROM THE JAPANESE-- PANICCIA-SAN.
YOU.
WHEN I GET THROUGH WITH YOU, YOU'RE--
NOW YOU CAN'T SAY I NEVER DO ANYTHING FOR YOU, HUH?
NO, NO! DON'T THANK ME YET!
THE BEST IS YET TO COME...

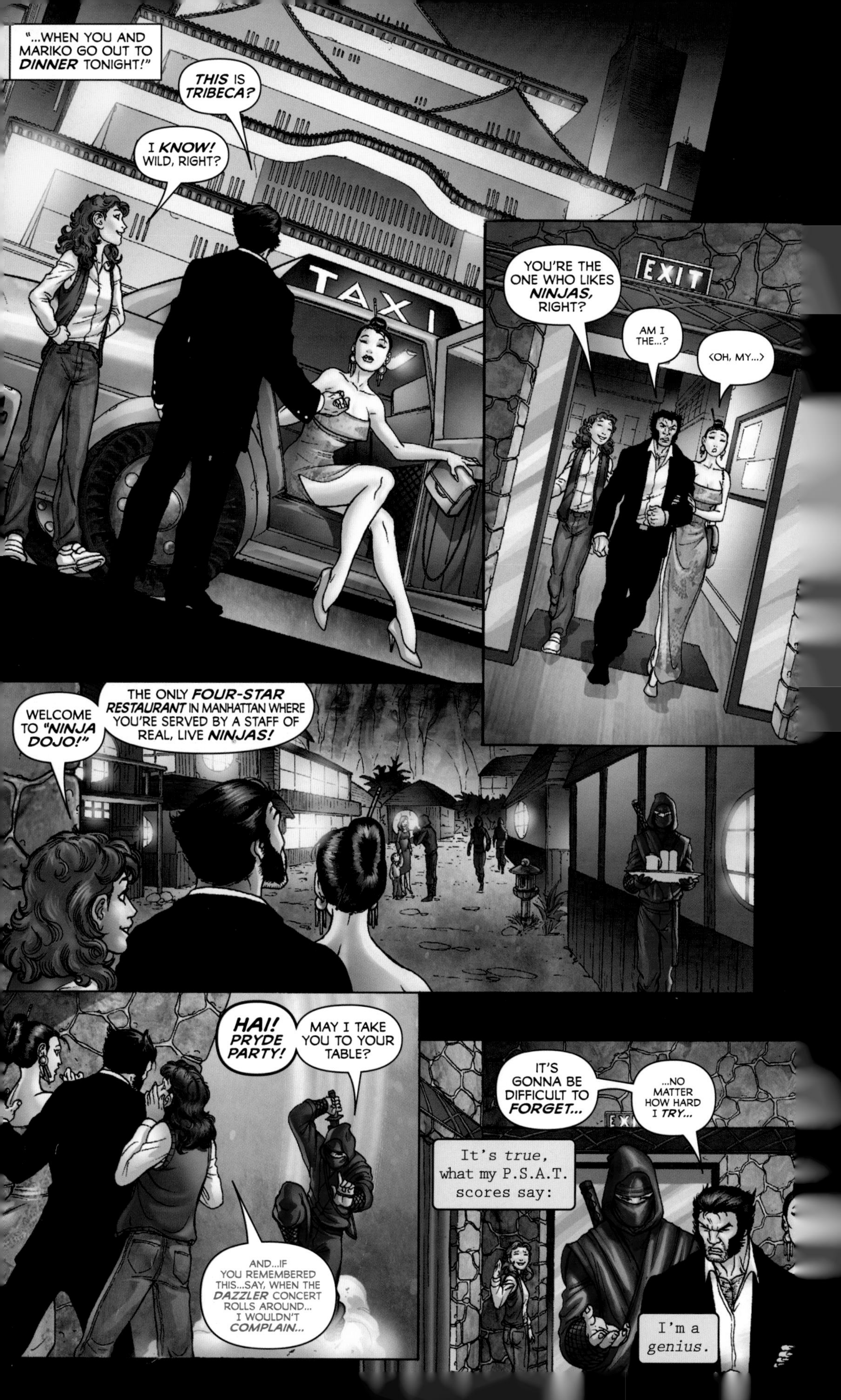
"...WHEN YOU AND MARIKO GO OUT TO DINNER TONIGHT!"
THIS IS TRIBECA?
I KNOW! WILD, RIGHT?
TAXI
YOU'RE THE ONE WHO LIKES NINJAS, RIGHT?
EXIT
AM I THE...?
<OH, MY...>
WELCOME TO "NINJA DOJO!"
THE ONLY FOUR-STAR RESTAURANT IN MANHATTAN WHERE YOU'RE SERVED BY A STAFF OF REAL, LIVE NINJAS!
HAI! PRYDE PARTY!
MAY I TAKE YOU TO YOUR TABLE?
AND...IF YOU REMEMBERED THIS...SAY, WHEN THE DAZZLER CONCERT ROLLS AROUND... I WOULDN'T COMPLAIN...
IT'S GONNA BE DIFFICULT TO FORGET...
...NO MATTER HOW HARD I TRY...
It's true, what my P.S.A.T. scores say:
I'm a genius.

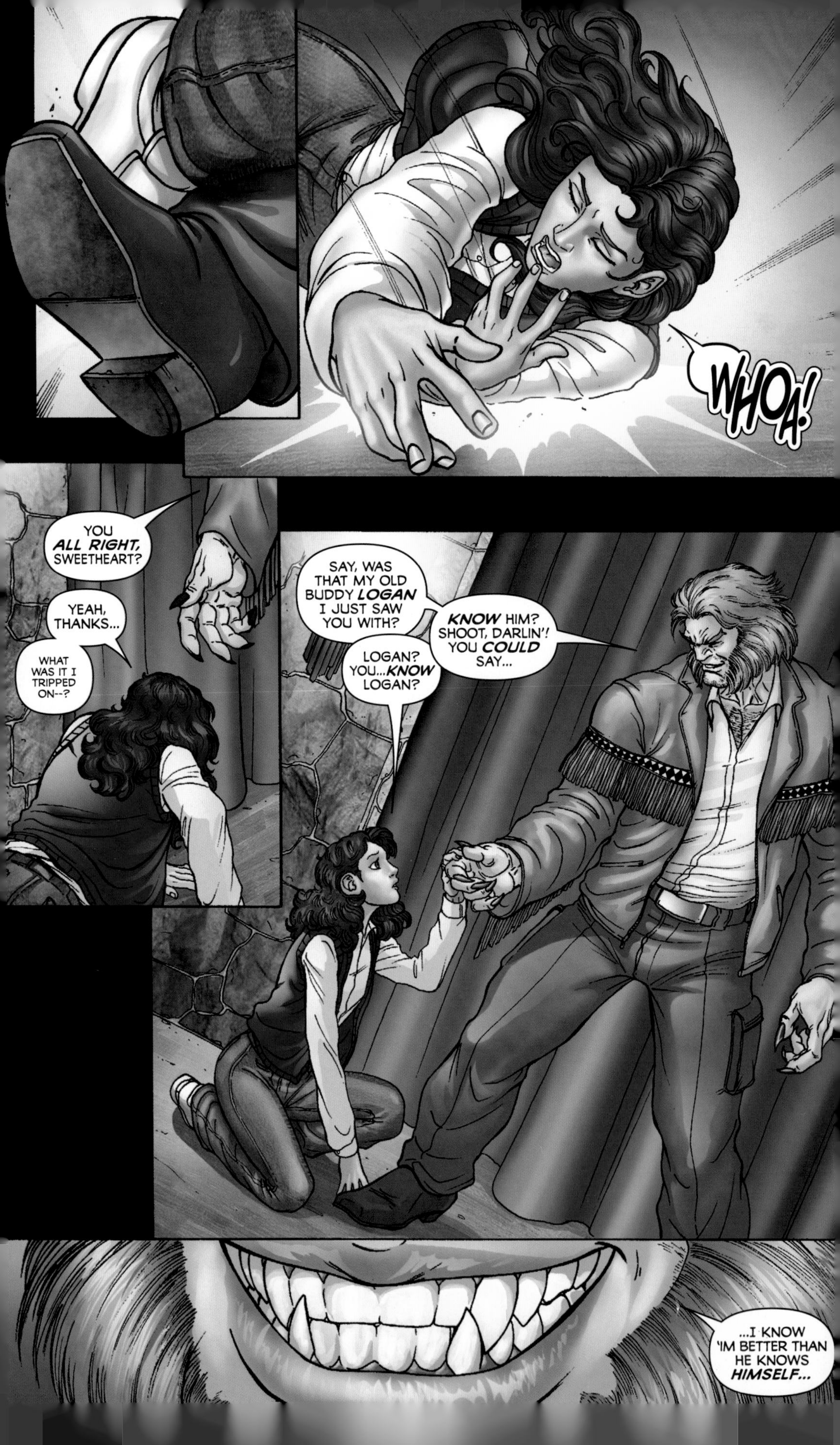
WHOA!
YOU ALL RIGHT, SWEETHEART?
YEAH, THANKS...
WHAT WAS IT I TRIPPED ON--?
SAY, WAS THAT MY OLD BUDDY LOGAN I JUST SAW YOU WITH?
LOGAN? YOU...KNOW LOGAN?
KNOW HIM? SHOOT, DARLIN'! YOU COULD SAY...
...I KNOW 'IM BETTER THAN HE KNOWS HIMSELF...

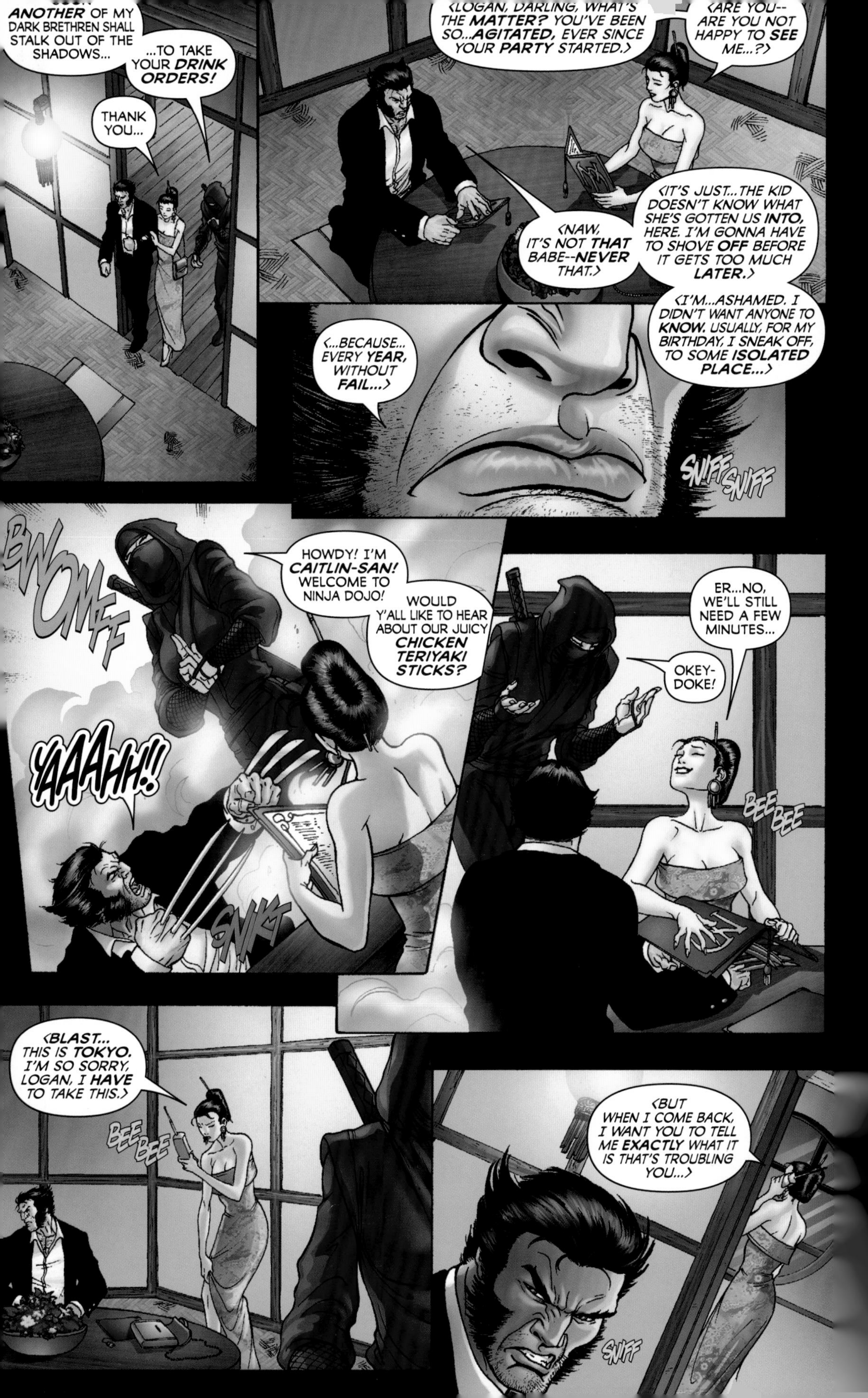

ANOTHER OF MY DARK BRETHREN SHALL STALK OUT OF THE SHADOWS...
...TO TAKE YOUR DRINK ORDERS!
THANK YOU...
‹LOGAN, DARLING, WHAT'S THE MATTER? YOU'VE BEEN SO...AGITATED, EVER SINCE YOUR PARTY STARTED.›
‹ARE YOU--ARE YOU NOT HAPPY TO SEE ME...?›
‹NAW, IT'S NOT THAT BABE--NEVER THAT.›
‹IT'S JUST...THE KID DOESN'T KNOW WHAT SHE'S GOTTEN US INTO, HERE. I'M GONNA HAVE TO SHOVE OFF BEFORE IT GETS TOO MUCH LATER.›
‹I'M...ASHAMED. I DIDN'T WANT ANYONE TO KNOW. USUALLY, FOR MY BIRTHDAY, I SNEAK OFF, TO SOME ISOLATED PLACE...›
‹...BECAUSE... EVERY YEAR, WITHOUT FAIL...›
SNIFF SNIFF
BWOMFF
HOWDY! I'M CAITLIN-SAN! WELCOME TO NINJA DOJO!
WOULD Y'ALL LIKE TO HEAR ABOUT OUR JUICY CHICKEN TERIYAKI STICKS?
YAAAHH!!
SNIKT
ER...NO, WE'LL STILL NEED A FEW MINUTES...
OKEY-DOKE!
BEE BEE
‹BLAST... THIS IS TOKYO. I'M SO SORRY, LOGAN, I HAVE TO TAKE THIS.›
BEE BEE
‹BUT WHEN I COME BACK, I WANT YOU TO TELL ME EXACTLY WHAT IT IS THAT'S TROUBLING YOU...›
SNIFF

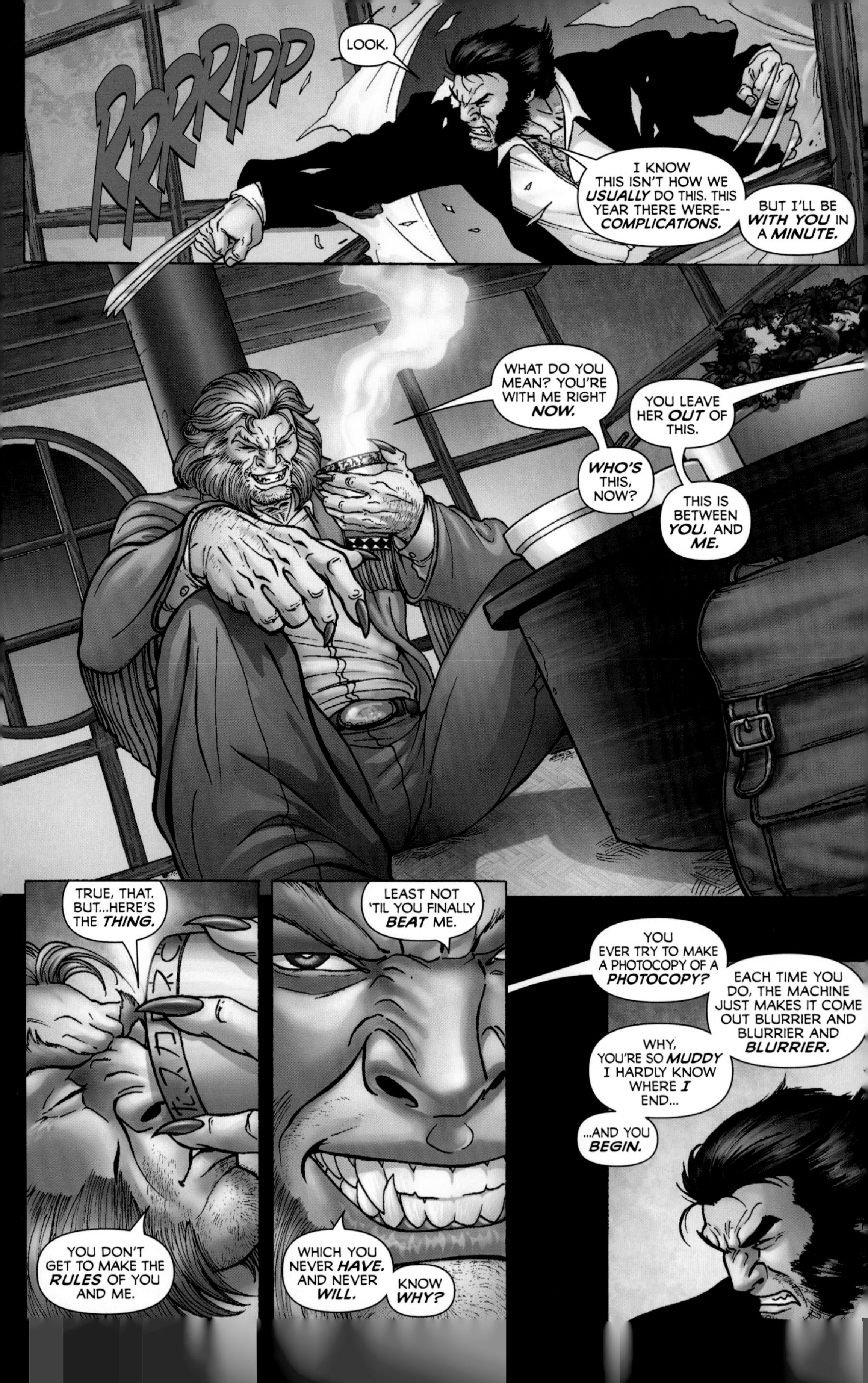
RRRRIPP
LOOK.
I KNOW THIS ISN'T HOW WE *USUALLY* DO THIS. THIS YEAR THERE WERE-- *COMPLICATIONS.*
BUT I'LL BE *WITH YOU* IN A *MINUTE.*
WHAT DO YOU MEAN? YOU'RE WITH ME RIGHT *NOW.*
WHO'S THIS, NOW?
YOU LEAVE HER *OUT* OF THIS.
THIS IS BETWEEN *YOU.* AND *ME.*
TRUE, THAT. BUT...HERE'S THE *THING.*
YOU DON'T GET TO MAKE THE *RULES* OF YOU AND ME.
LEAST NOT 'TIL YOU FINALLY *BEAT* ME.
WHICH YOU NEVER *HAVE.* AND NEVER *WILL.*
KNOW *WHY?*
YOU EVER TRY TO MAKE A PHOTOCOPY OF A *PHOTOCOPY?*
EACH TIME YOU DO, THE MACHINE JUST MAKES IT COME OUT BLURRIER AND BLURRIER AND *BLURRIER.*
WHY, YOU'RE SO *MUDDY* I HARDLY KNOW WHERE *I* END...
...AND YOU *BEGIN.*

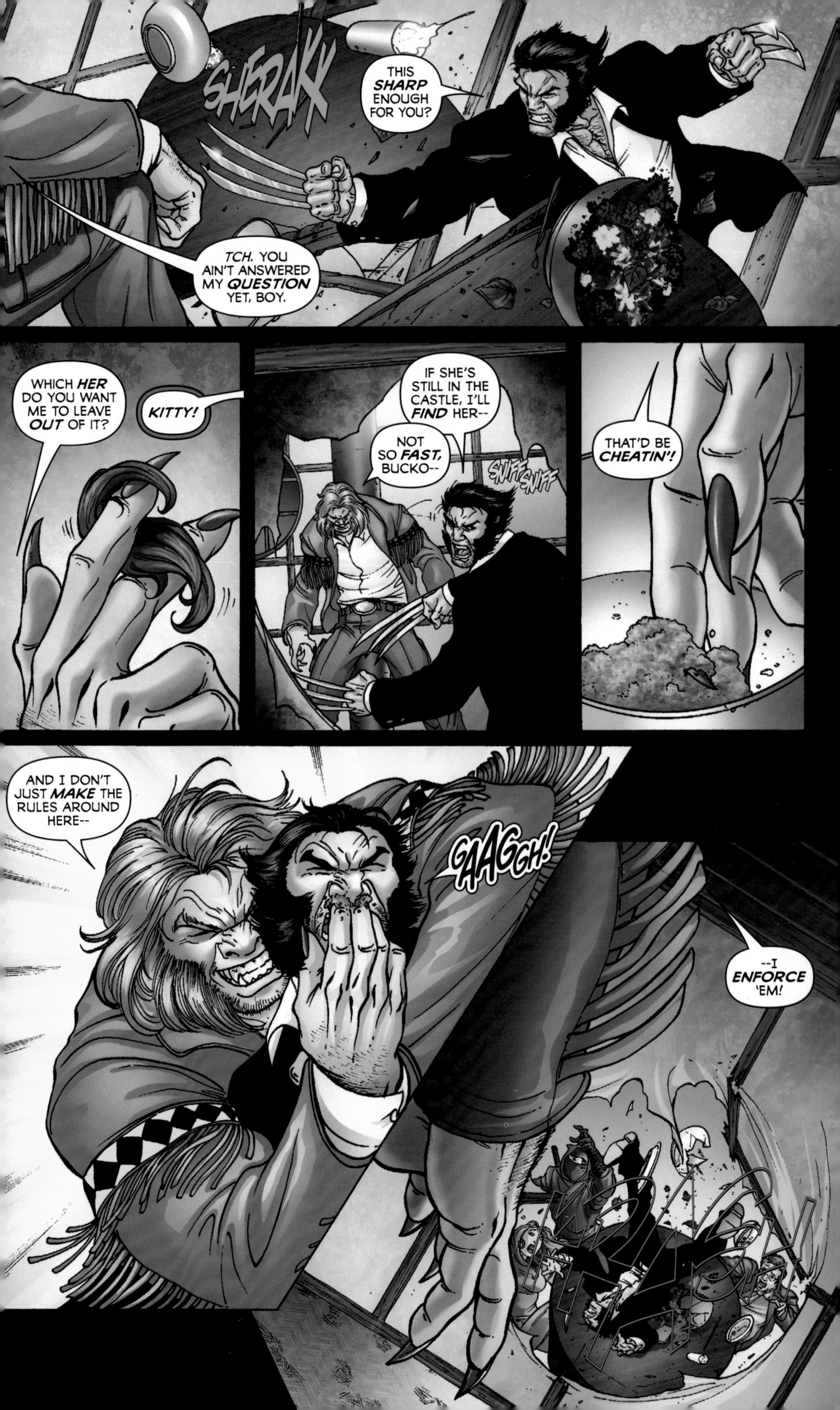
SHERAKK
THIS SHARP ENOUGH FOR YOU?
TCH. YOU AIN'T ANSWERED MY QUESTION YET, BOY.
WHICH HER DO YOU WANT ME TO LEAVE OUT OF IT?
KITTY!
IF SHE'S STILL IN THE CASTLE, I'LL FIND HER--
NOT SO FAST, BUCKO--
SNIFF SNIFF
THAT'D BE CHEATIN'!
AND I DON'T JUST MAKE THE RULES AROUND HERE--
GAAGGH!
--I ENFORCE 'EM!

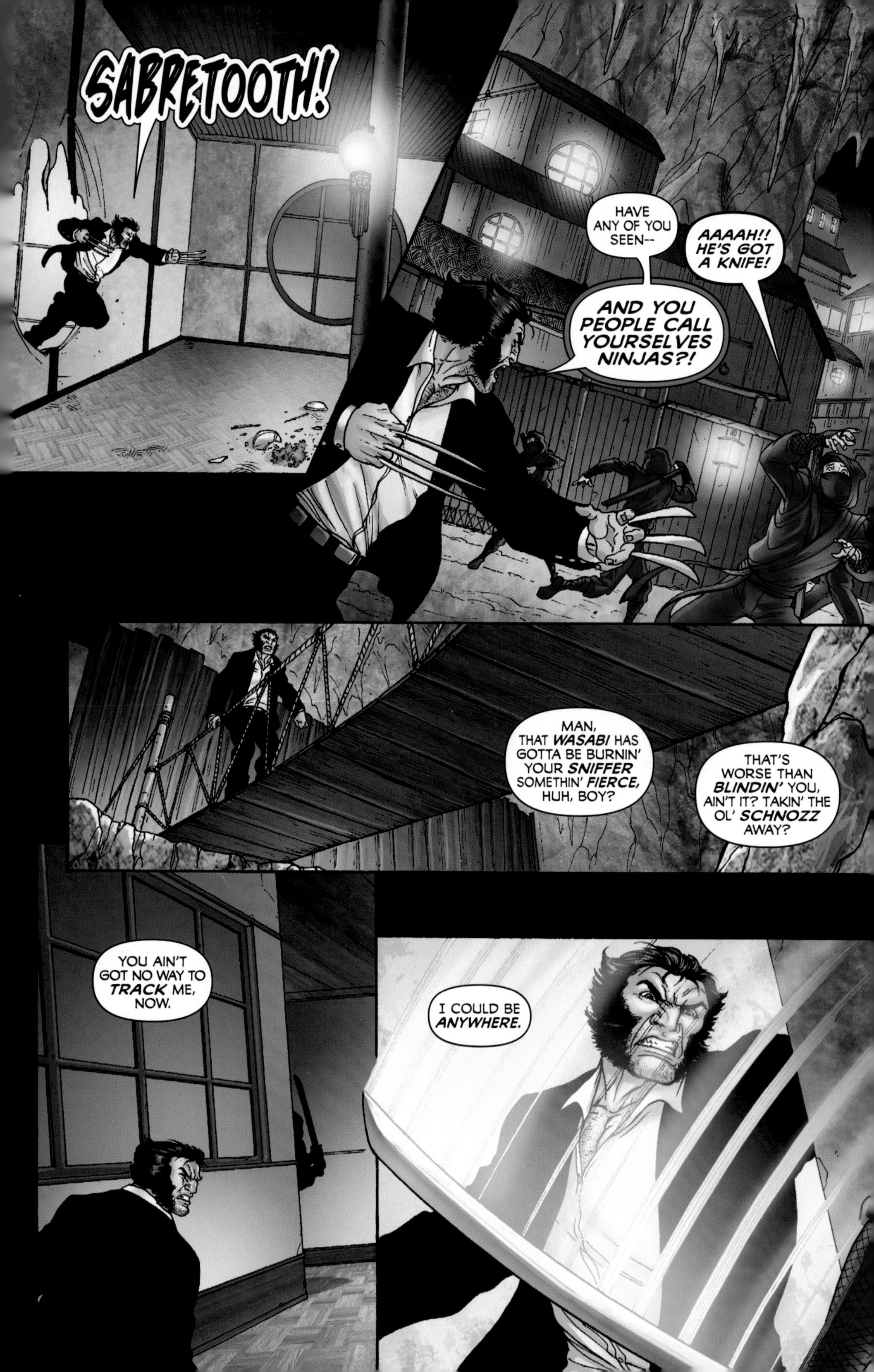
SABRETOOTH!
HAVE ANY OF YOU SEEN--
AND YOU PEOPLE CALL YOURSELVES NINJAS?!
AAAAH!! HE'S GOT A KNIFE!
MAN, THAT WASABI HAS GOTTA BE BURNIN' YOUR SNIFFER SOMETHIN' FIERCE, HUH, BOY?
THAT'S WORSE THAN BLINDIN' YOU, AIN'T IT? TAKIN' THE OL' SCHNOZZ AWAY?
YOU AIN'T GOT NO WAY TO TRACK ME, NOW.
I COULD BE ANYWHERE.

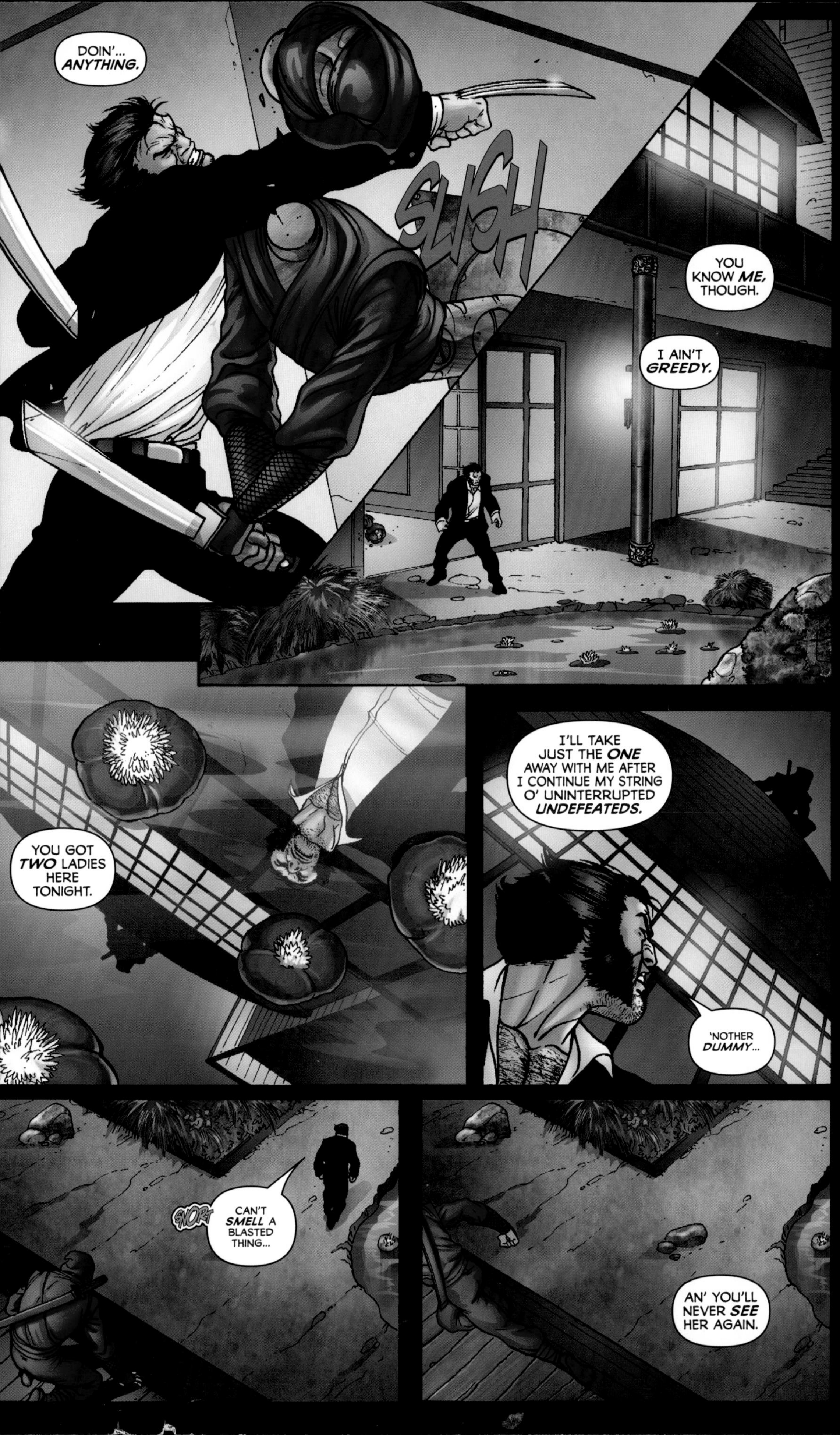
DOIN'... ANYTHING.
SLISH
YOU KNOW ME, THOUGH.
I AIN'T GREEDY.
YOU GOT TWO LADIES HERE TONIGHT.
I'LL TAKE JUST THE ONE AWAY WITH ME AFTER I CONTINUE MY STRING O' UNINTERRUPTED UNDEFEATEDS.
'NOTHER DUMMY...
SNORT
CAN'T SMELL A BLASTED THING...
AN' YOU'LL NEVER SEE HER AGAIN.

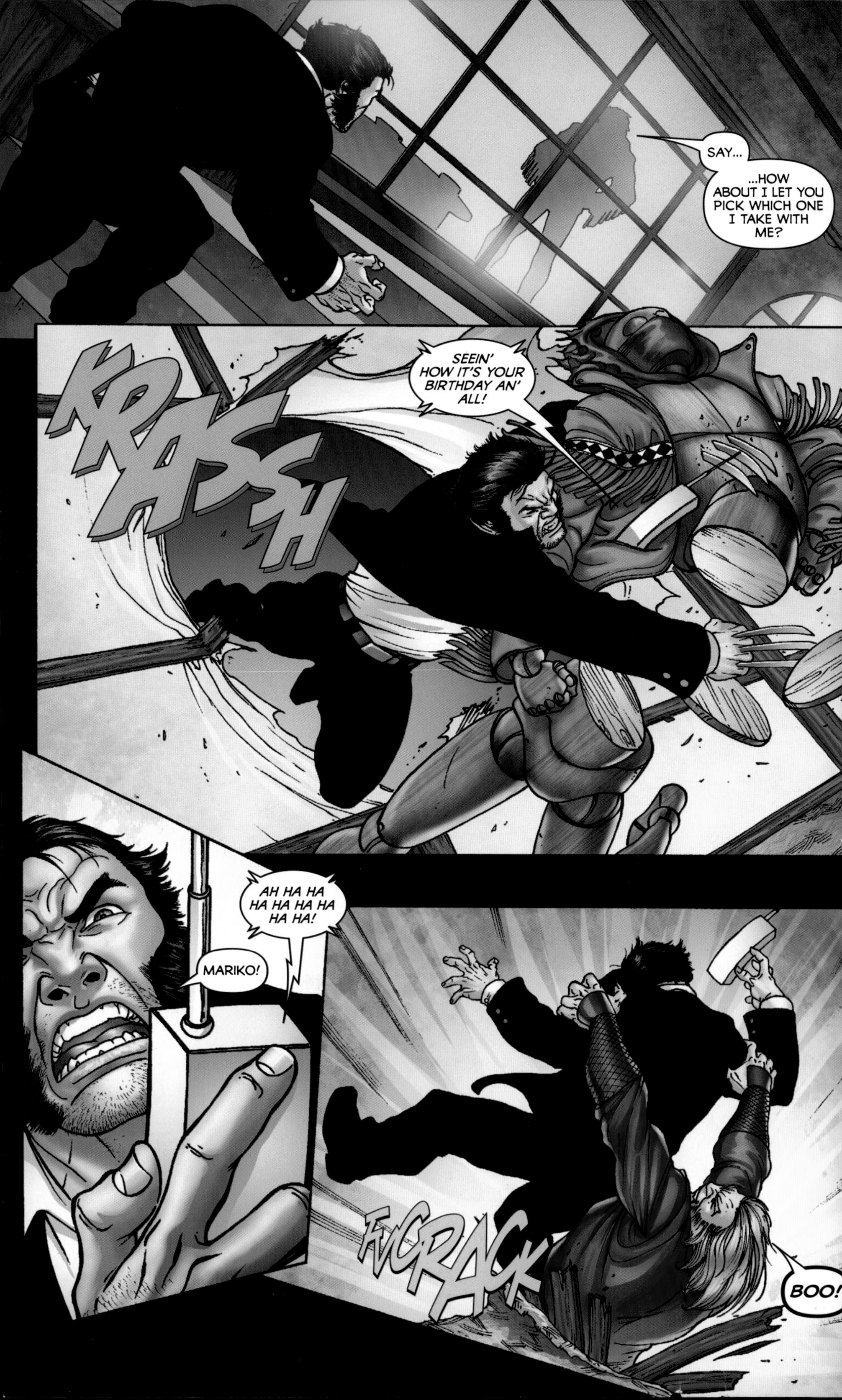
SAY...
...HOW ABOUT I LET YOU PICK WHICH ONE I TAKE WITH ME?
KRASH
SEEIN' HOW IT'S YOUR BIRTHDAY AN' ALL!
MARIKO!
AH HA HA HA HA HA HA HA HA!
FVCRACK
BOO!

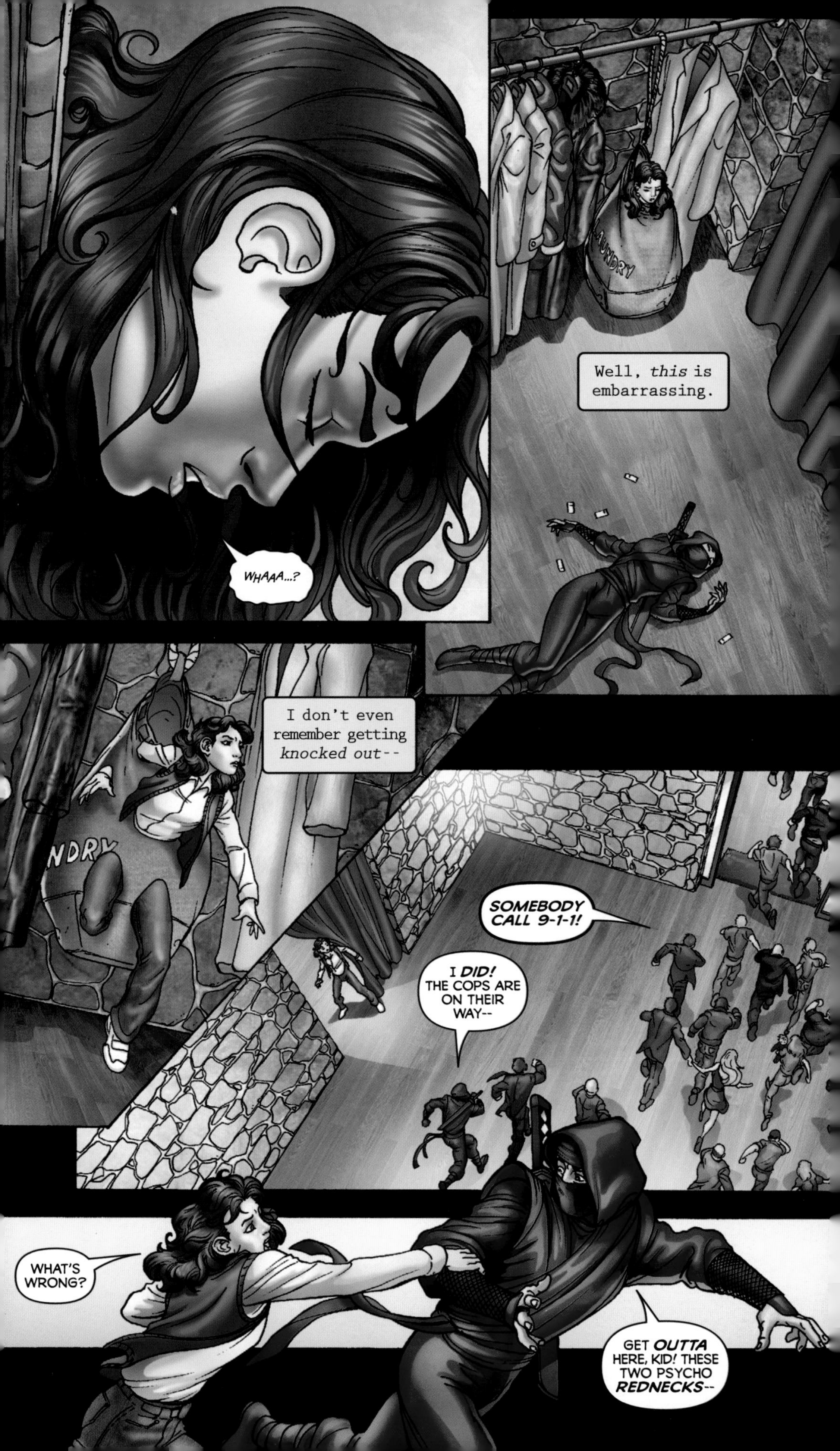

WHAAA...?
Well, *this* is embarrassing.
LAUNDRY
I don't even remember getting *knocked out*--
NDRY
SOMEBODY CALL 9-1-1!
I *DID!* THE COPS ARE ON THEIR WAY--
WHAT'S WRONG?
GET *OUTTA* HERE, KID! THESE TWO PSYCHO *REDNECKS*--

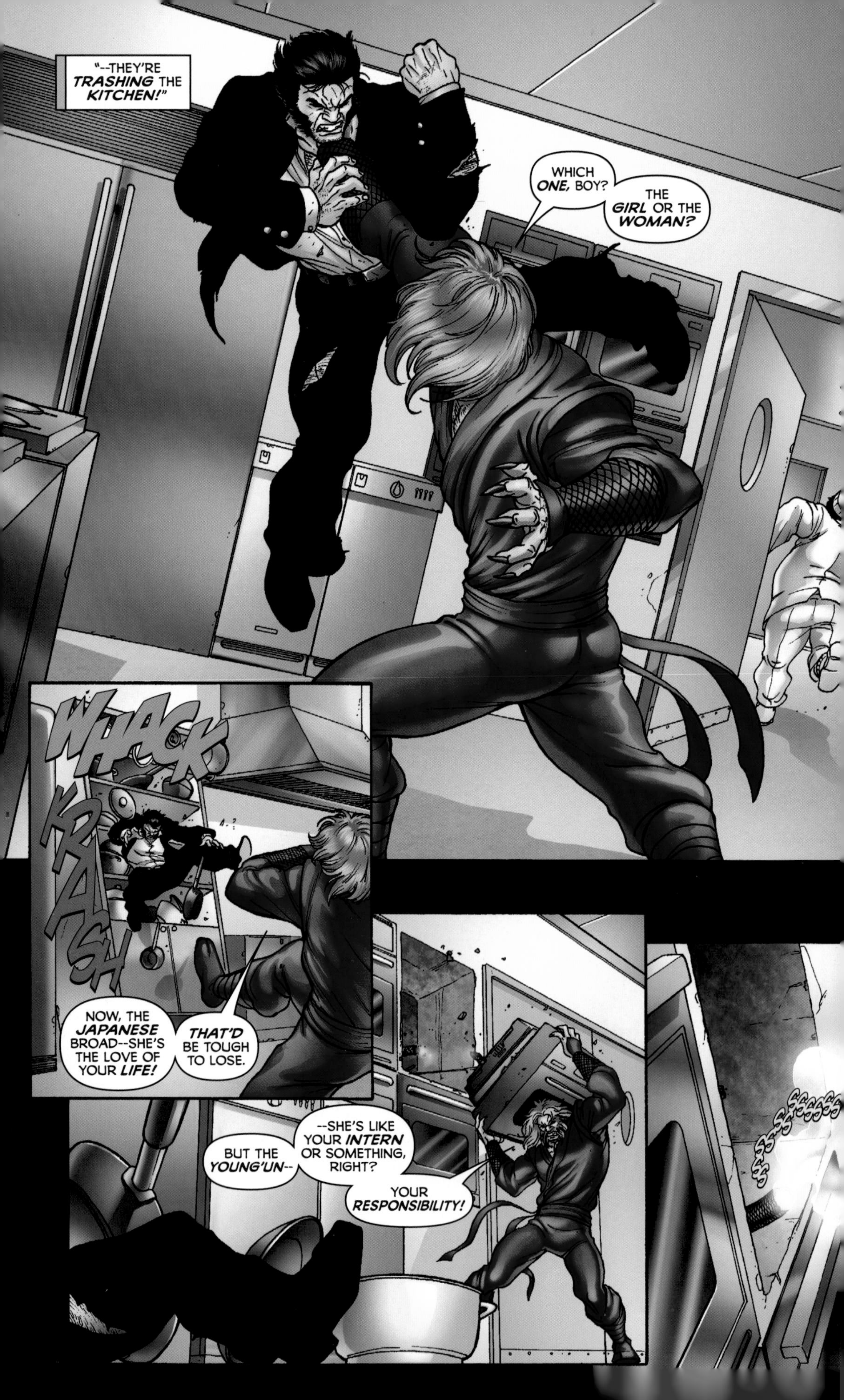
"--THEY'RE TRASHING THE KITCHEN!"
WHICH ONE, BOY?
THE GIRL OR THE WOMAN?
WHACK
KRASH
NOW, THE JAPANESE BROAD--SHE'S THE LOVE OF YOUR LIFE!
THAT'D BE TOUGH TO LOSE.
BUT THE YOUNG'UN--
--SHE'S LIKE YOUR INTERN OR SOMETHING, RIGHT?
YOUR RESPONSIBILITY!

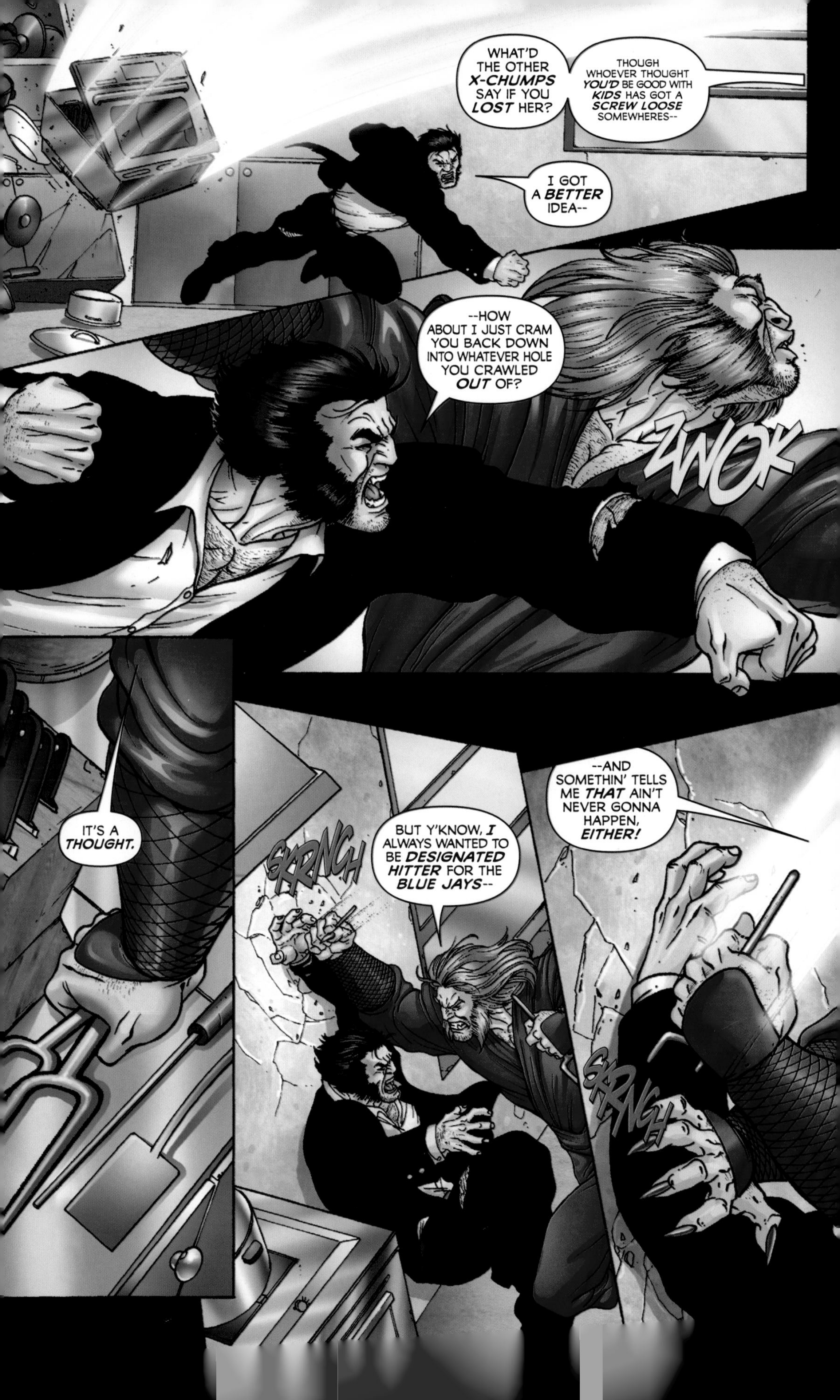
WHAT'D THE OTHER X-CHUMPS SAY IF YOU LOST HER?
THOUGH WHOEVER THOUGHT YOU'D BE GOOD WITH KIDS HAS GOT A SCREW LOOSE SOMEWHERES--
I GOT A BETTER IDEA--
--HOW ABOUT I JUST CRAM YOU BACK DOWN INTO WHATEVER HOLE YOU CRAWLED OUT OF?
ZWOK
IT'S A THOUGHT.
SKRNCH
BUT Y'KNOW, I ALWAYS WANTED TO BE DESIGNATED HITTER FOR THE BLUE JAYS--
--AND SOMETHIN' TELLS ME THAT AIN'T NEVER GONNA HAPPEN, EITHER!
SKRNCH

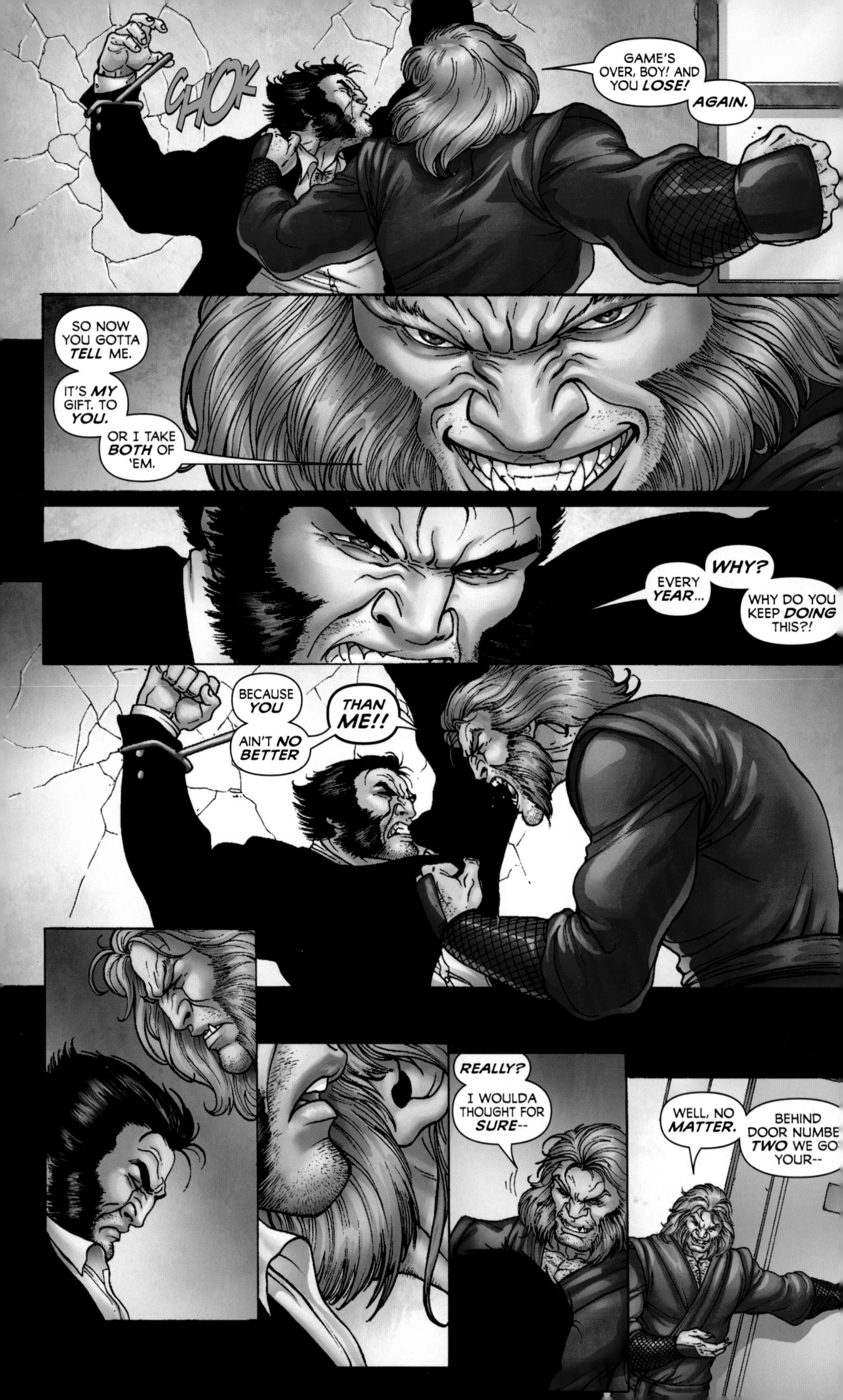

CHOK
GAME'S OVER, BOY! AND YOU LOSE!
AGAIN.
SO NOW YOU GOTTA TELL ME.
IT'S MY GIFT. TO YOU.
OR I TAKE BOTH OF 'EM.
EVERY YEAR...
WHY?
WHY DO YOU KEEP DOING THIS?!
BECAUSE YOU
AIN'T NO BETTER
THAN ME!!
REALLY?
I WOULDA THOUGHT FOR SURE--
WELL, NO MATTER.
BEHIND DOOR NUMBE TWO WE GO YOUR--

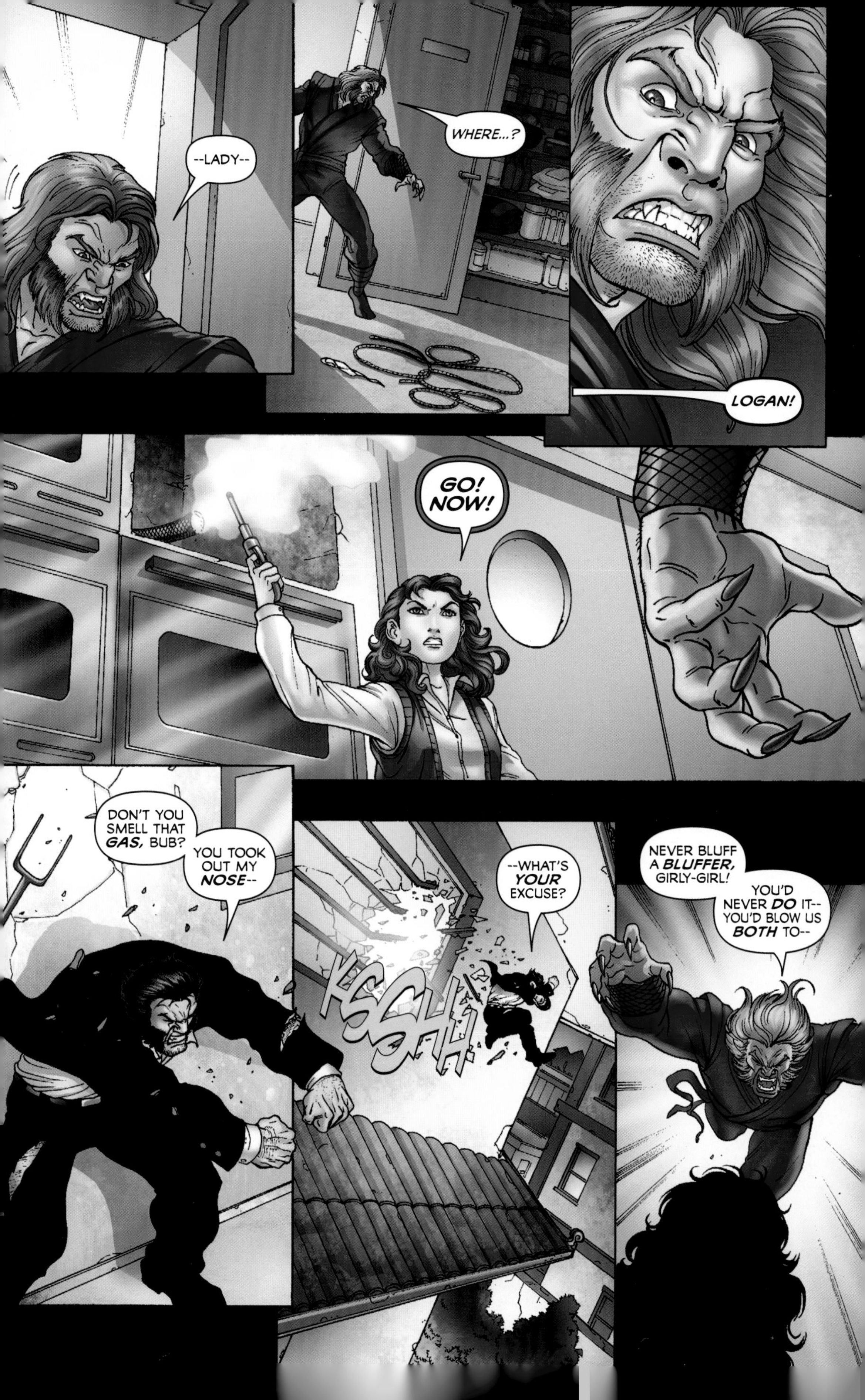
--LADY--
WHERE...?
LOGAN!
GO! NOW!
DON'T YOU SMELL THAT GAS, BUB?
YOU TOOK OUT MY NOSE--
--WHAT'S YOUR EXCUSE?
KSSHH
NEVER BLUFF A BLUFFER, GIRLY-GIRL!
YOU'D NEVER DO IT-- YOU'D BLOW US BOTH TO--

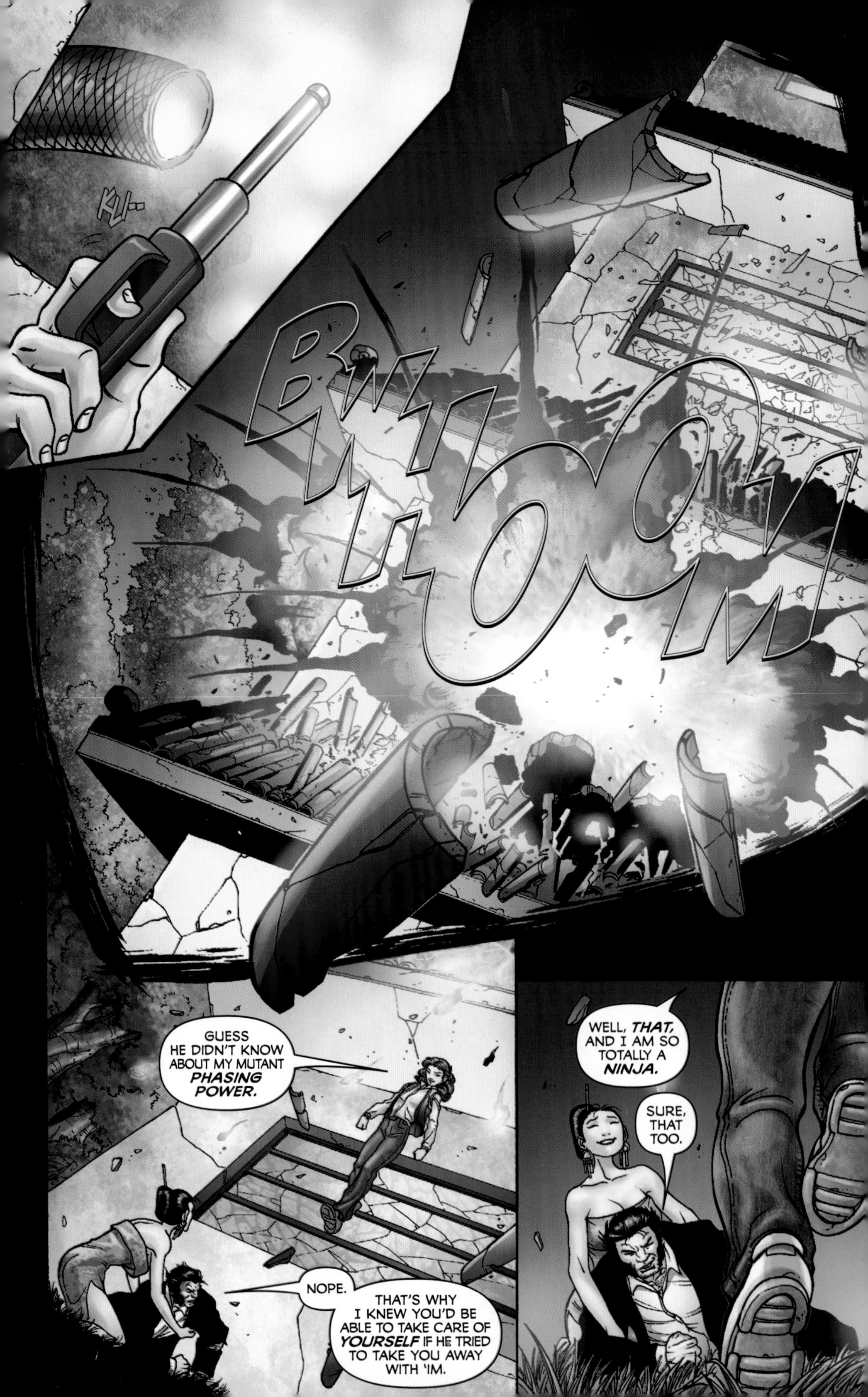
KLIK
BWHOOM
GUESS HE DIDN'T KNOW ABOUT MY MUTANT *PHASING POWER.*
NOPE.
THAT'S WHY I KNEW YOU'D BE ABLE TO TAKE CARE OF *YOURSELF* IF HE TRIED TO TAKE YOU AWAY WITH 'IM.
WELL, *THAT,* AND I AM SO TOTALLY A *NINJA.*
SURE, THAT TOO.

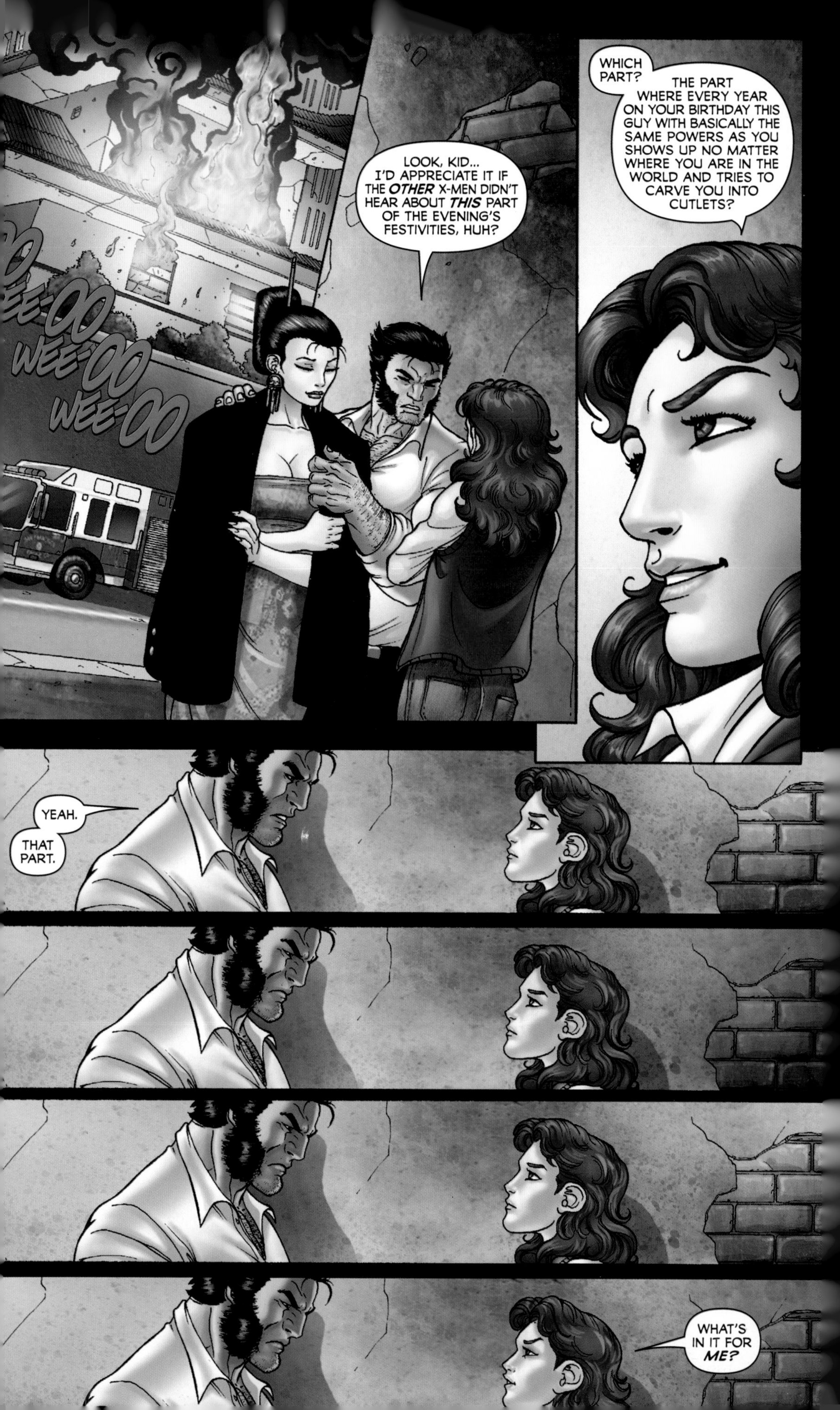

WEE-OO
WEE-OO
WEE-OO
WEE-OO
LOOK, KID... I'D APPRECIATE IT IF THE OTHER X-MEN DIDN'T HEAR ABOUT THIS PART OF THE EVENING'S FESTIVITIES, HUH?
WHICH PART?
THE PART WHERE EVERY YEAR ON YOUR BIRTHDAY THIS GUY WITH BASICALLY THE SAME POWERS AS YOU SHOWS UP NO MATTER WHERE YOU ARE IN THE WORLD AND TRIES TO CARVE YOU INTO CUTLETS?
YEAH.
THAT PART.
WHAT'S IN IT FOR ME?

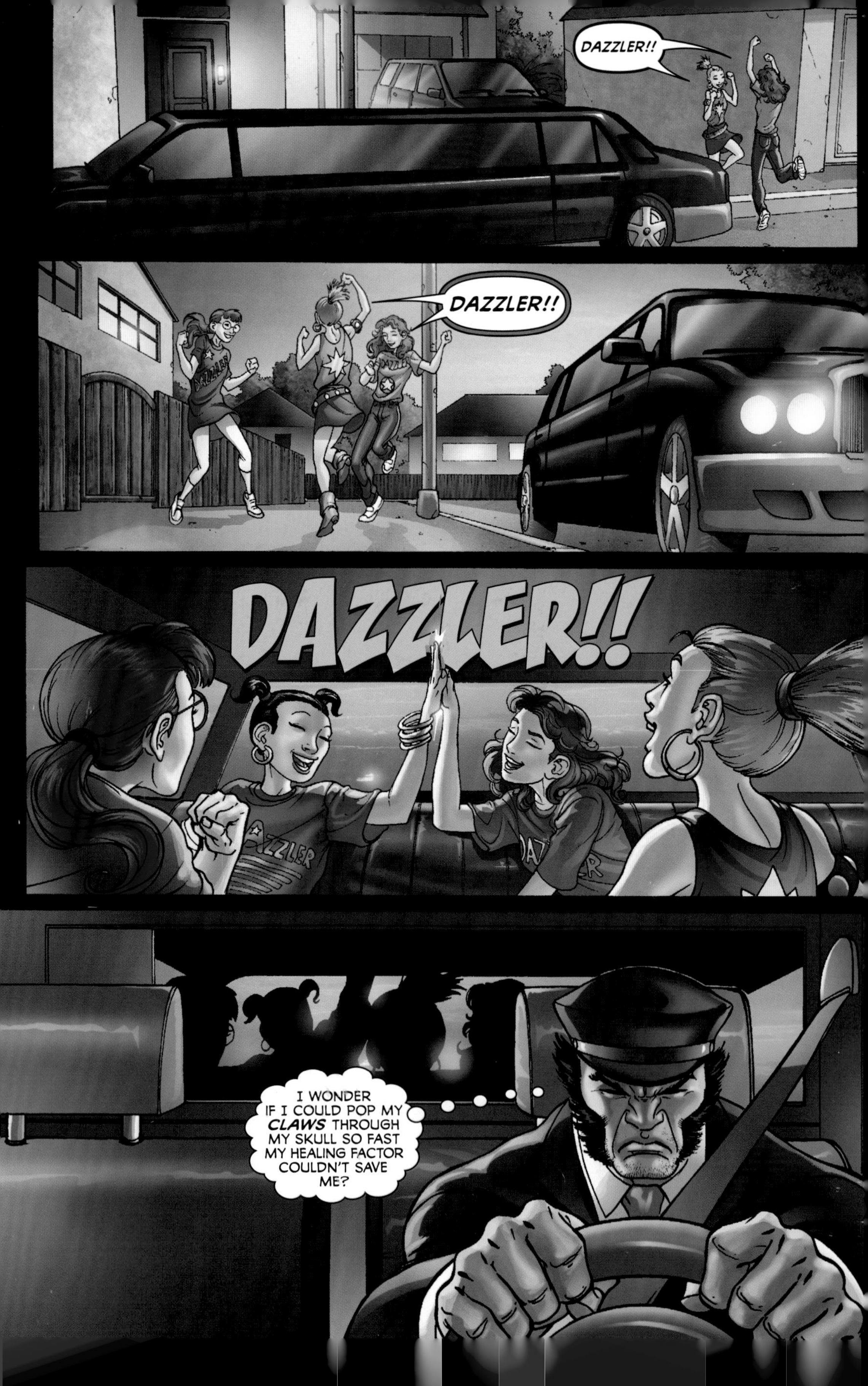
DAZZLER!!
DAZZLER!!
DAZZLER!!
I WONDER IF I COULD POP MY CLAWS THROUGH MY SKULL SO FAST MY HEALING FACTOR COULDN'T SAVE ME?